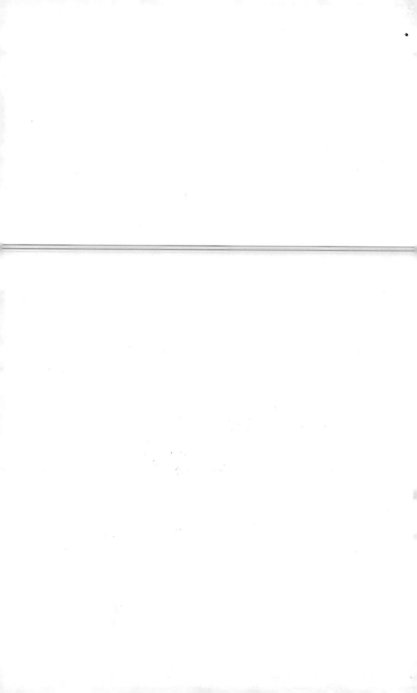

FOOTBALL
NIGHTMARE

MATT CHRISTOPHER

The #1 Sports Series for Kids

FOOTBALL NIGHTMARE

Text by Robert Hirschfeld

Little, Brown and Company
Boston   New York   London

AR
4.7

First Edition

Matt Christopher™ is a trademark of Catherine M. Christopher.

Text by Robert Hirschfeld

Library of Congress Cataloging-in-Publication Data

Hirschfeld, Robert.
    Football nightmare : the #1 sports series for kids / Matt Chris-
topher ; text by Robert Hirschfeld. — 1st ed.
        p.   cm.
    Summary: Having dropped a pass and made his football team miss
having an undefeated season, thirteen-year-old Keith fears that he
will continue to make bad mistakes and wonders if he should continue playing football.
    ISBN 0-316-14370-7 (hc) / ISBN 0-316-14307-3 (pb)
    [1. Football — Fiction.   2. Fear — Fiction.]   I. Christopher,
Matt.   II. Title.
PZ7.H59794 Fo   2001
[Fic] — dc21   00-054607

10 9 8 7 6 5 4 3 2

COM-MO

Printed in the United States of America

1

"**D**EE-*fense! Dee-fense! DEE-fense!*"

The crowd's screaming was beginning to sound desperate, Keith Stedman thought, as he stood on the sideline and checked the clock for about the millionth time in the last few minutes. The clock didn't show good news.

There was exactly one minute and ten seconds left in the game. Seventy ticks of the clock — and Keith's team, the Bucks, trailed by four points, 21–17.

All the opposing team, the Renegades, had to do was grind out another first down, and that would be that. Bye-bye, victory; so long, championship; farewell, undefeated season.

Hello, wait until next year.

Keith wondered if losing got any easier with time. He doubted it.

The Renegade fullback plunged into the line and picked up three yards. The Buck coach, Greg Bodie, signaled for a time-out, which meant that they were down to only one. Across the field, the Renegade fans were jumping up and down and high-fiving each other.

Keith turned and looked up into the bleachers behind him. His parents and little sister, Traci, were there. Mr. Stedman looked grim, and even nine-year-old Traci, who knew roughly as much about football as she did about nuclear physics, wore an unhappy expression on her freckled face.

Next to him, Keith's best buddy, Heck Szymanski, kicked the turf and muttered to himself. Heck was the Buck's top running back, with great balance and the ability to shift into high gear and leave defenses in the dust . . . when the offense had the ball. Keith was a rangy wide receiver who knew how to run a good pattern. But neither of them could do their thing when they were standing helpless on the sideline while the clock ticked away.

"If we could just get one more shot at it," said Heck. "We could beat these guys, I *know* it."

Keith sighed and nodded glumly. "Yeah . . . *if*. But you know they're not going to throw any passes or laterals."

"Not unless the quarterback suddenly goes crazy," agreed Heck. "The only chance we have is if they fumble and —"

Heck's next words were drowned out by a roar from the Buck fans. Startled, both boys stared out on the field. While they had been talking, the Renegades had put the ball in play.

And they had *fumbled!* The fullback had failed to hang on to the handoff from the quarterback and the ball had squirted loose. A pile of players lay tangled together, some in red Buck jerseys and some in green Renegade ones. Somewhere under the pile was the ball. The referee began moving the players away while Keith and Heck watched and held their breath.

Finally the ref picked up the ball and signaled that it now belonged to the Bucks.

"*YES!*" screamed Heck, as the Buck offense raced out on the field. Coach Bodie grabbed Billy Brundage, the Buck quarterback, and gave him some last-minute instructions.

As they huddled, tackle Cody Aarons clenched a fist and shook it. "We can *do* it!" he yelled.

But Keith knew it wouldn't be easy, not with under a minute left and only one time-out to use. A field goal wouldn't do it; the Bucks needed a touchdown. And they were sixty-five yards away from pay dirt.

Billy Brundage began by whipping a pass to Warren Flatt, the tight end. Warren ploughed ahead for twelve yards before lunging out of bounds to stop the clock.

Then Billy dropped back, faked a handoff that fooled nobody on the defense — everyone knew that Billy had to air it out — and tossed a swing pass to Heck out on the flat. Cody threw a smashing downfield block and Heck tightroped down the sideline for a gain of nine. The ball was now on the Renegade forty-four, but the clock showed just twenty seconds left.

The Bucks lined up fast. Billy called for a play that sent Keith deep on a fly pattern while Warren went over the middle. After the snap, Keith sped downfield, but a Renegade safety stayed with him step for step. Billy had to throw to the tight end, who got the first down with yards to spare, but was unable to get out of bounds. The Bucks burned their final time-out.

The ball was on the Renegade thirty-eight yard line; there were only nine seconds remaining. Billy trotted off to talk to the coach. The Buck fans were screaming for a score, and now it was the Renegade rooters' turn to call for *"DEE-fense."*

Billy ran back on the field and the Bucks huddled.

"Listen up," he said. "We're gonna try the half-back option. Keith, you're going long again. Heck, think you can throw it?"

Heck nodded. "Sure. And you *know* Keith can catch it."

Keith felt his pulse racing and tried to stay calm. The halfback option meant that Billy would lateral to Heck and hope that the Buck defense would converge on him, looking for a run. Heck would draw the defense in, and Keith would be able to get free downfield. Then Heck would toss him the ball, and Keith would take it in for the winning TD.

Billy looked at his teammates. "This is it," he said. "You guys on the line, you gotta hold off those rushers and give this a chance to develop."

5

"Don't worry about us," Cody said. "We'll be there."

The ref whistled. The clock started.

"Okay," Billy said. "On *two*. Let's go!"

The Bucks ran up to the line and Keith split out to the left. The noise was deafening, especially from the Renegade fans trying to drown out Billy's signals.

"Set!" Billy yelled, his voice just audible over the roar. "*Hut* one! *Hut* two!"

Keith concentrated on his assignment and on keeping his breathing steady. On the snap, he took off downfield. Sure enough, he saw the safety who should have stayed with him move toward the line of scrimmage, looking for a run. By the time the guy realized that it might be a pass after all, Keith had ten yards on him.

There were no green jerseys anywhere near Keith as he looked back for Heck's pass.

And here it came, a little wobbly, but right on target. Keith watched the ball arc right toward his waiting hands — a perfectly aimed pass. All he had to do was pull it down and trot into the end zone untouched. The game was theirs, and so was the championship.

The ball hit his hands . . .

. . . and slid out of his hands and bounced on the field.

The Buck fans' happy screams stopped as if they had been cut off by a switch.

Keith lunged forward, as if he could somehow grab the ball and save the day. He hit the turf and lay there motionless, vaguely aware that the cheering was now coming from the Renegade bleachers.

Keith didn't want to get up. He didn't want to face his teammates, or his family, or anybody at all. It was definitely the worst moment of his life.

Dimly Keith heard the gun sound and he knew that the game was over. He felt like a lot more had ended than just a game . . . football was over, fun was over . . . *everything* was over.

2

Keith was helping his father clear away the dishes from the table after dinner when the doorbell rang.

"I'll get it," Traci called out as she raced for the door.

It was a warm evening in late August. Nine months had passed since Keith had dropped the pass. By now, whole days could go by without Keith dreaming or thinking about the awful moment. His parents and sister had learned not to bring it up, so Keith felt safe from being reminded of that game while he was in the house — unless he dreamed about it. There was no way to control what his brain did when he was asleep.

The weeks after that game had been rough on Keith. Some photographer from the local newspaper had taken a shot of him lying flat on the field after blowing the catch. The caption under the picture had read "The agony of defeat," which, Keith felt, pretty much said it all. There had been an article about the game, which Keith had not read. He didn't need to read it. He had been there.

Most of the other Bucks had made a point of supporting Keith after the game and ever since then, especially Heck, Cody, and Billy. Heck said over and over that it could have just as easily happened to him, or to anyone. Keith finally had told his friend to just not bring it up anymore, and Heck had agreed, though he wasn't happy about it.

But a few guys on the team, and some kids who were not on the team, and even a few adults had said nasty things. Keith was certain that many still were saying them — behind his back, of course.

He imagined that when some of his teammates were old men, they'd tell their grandchildren about the time the Bucks could have been champs, *would* have been champs, except that this guy, Keith Stedman, had blown a sure touchdown.

He'd have to live with this for the rest of his life, he knew. And he didn't want to talk about it or think about it or do anything that might remind him of it.

Was that asking too much?

"Keith!" Traci ran into the kitchen. "It's Heck and Mr. Bodie! They want to talk to you!"

Ignoring his father's puzzled expression, Keith slowly moped out of the kitchen and into the living room, where his friend and the Bucks' coach waited. They both smiled at Keith, who didn't return their smiles with one of his own.

"Hey, bud!" Heck extended his hand for a low-five. "Haven't seen much of you lately. Where have you been, anyway?"

Keith noticed that his parents had come into the room. Keith managed not to groan out loud, but he knew this was going to be bad.

"How are you, Keith? Mr. Stedman?" the coach asked.

"Okay, I guess," Keith muttered.

"Hi, Heck," said Mr. Stedman. "Coach Bodie, good to see you. Heck, would you like some home-made peach pie? Coach, how about you?"

"No thanks," the coach replied, and even Heck shook his head. Heck had never turned down dessert of any kind. Keith shifted from foot to foot.

"The thing is," Coach Bodie began, "the Bucks

are gearing up for the new season. We had our first team meeting this afternoon, and I'd been hoping to see you there, Keith."

"Yeah, me too," added Heck. "We *need* you, dude. You're a major weapon, you know?"

"There was a team meeting today?" Mr. Stedman asked. He turned to face Keith. "This is the first I've heard of it. Did you know about this, son?"

Keith felt embarrassed and nodded. "Yeah. I got a card about it last week, but . . ." He trailed off, not wanting to continue.

Mr. Stedman wasn't going to let it drop like that. "But what? How come you didn't even mention this to us?"

Keith's mouth felt dry and he coughed. He saw his parents exchange a worried frown and looked down at the floor, not wanting to meet anyone's eyes.

"I was thinking I didn't feel like playing this year, that's all. It's no big deal."

"Honey, are you absolutely sure?" asked Keith's mother. "You've always loved sports, and especially football."

"Yeah, well, I can change my mind, can't I? People change their minds, right?"

There was a long, awkward silence, which the coach finally broke.

"If you don't want to play, Keith, that's your decision to make, of course. But I'm sorry to hear it, and the team will be sorry too. I was counting on your being our top wide receiver."

Keith continued to stare at the ground. "Yeah, right," he mumbled.

Mr. Stedman leaned forward. "Keith? Look at me, son."

Slowly, reluctantly, Keith raised his eyes to meet his father's. "Listen, Keith. . . . What happened in that last game wasn't that big a deal. People make mistakes, and they go on from there. I'd hate to see you give up something that was important to you just because you made a mistake."

"It wasn't just any mistake!" Keith blurted. "It was a *huge* mistake! It cost us the game and the title! It was on the front page of the *paper!*"

Heck jumped in. "Yeah, but . . . listen, the Renegade fullback? The guy that fumbled? *He* was almost the goat! If we'd scored, it would have been him, right? That's just the way these things happen.

If we'd had another couple of minutes, we still might have scored and nobody would remember you ever dropped — I mean, it wouldn't have mattered."

"But it *did* matter," Keith snapped. "It mattered a lot, and it *still* matters. People are still ragging me about it."

"Who?" Heck demanded. "Point them out to me and I'll straighten them out, fast."

Keith started pacing back and forth. "It doesn't matter who. Look, you don't get it. It didn't happen to you, so you couldn't understand. Dad, remember the story you told me? About that baseball player?"

"Which player?" Mr. Stedman looked puzzled. "Oh, you mean Fred Merkle?"

"Yeah," Keith replied. He looked at Heck. "This guy, Merkle, played Major League baseball a long time ago, and he was good, too. But he made one mistake in a big game, just *one*. And no one ever let him forget it. For the rest of his life, people called him 'Bonehead' Merkle. Right, Dad?"

Mr. Stedman sighed. "Right. But —"

"Right!" Keith cut him off. "It didn't matter that

he was a good ballplayer, batted .300, was a good fielder. For the rest of his life, he was 'Bonehead' Merkle of the New York Giants."

"That was different, son," said Mr. Stedman softly. "That was the Major Leagues, and he was a pro . . . and it was still unfair. But nobody expects a boy to never make mistakes."

"I don't see it that way. I don't want to have to listen to people give me grief about that for the rest of *my* life. So I'll find something else to do, something that's not football."

"Listen," Heck said, "if you'd just talk to the guys on the team, you'd see that they all want you back and that nobody blames you for what happened. And if there are one or two creeps somewhere who give you grief, well, who cares what they say? Your buddies know that you're a great ballplayer, a great pass-catcher."

"I think you should do whatever you decide," Mrs. Stedman said, putting a hand on her son's shoulder. "But I hate to think that you'll be unhappy, not being out there with your friends."

"Keith?" His sister, Traci, had come into the room and heard part of the conversation. She had an anxious look on her face. "Is that true? You aren't going to play football anymore?"

"Right," said Keith.

"You won't change your mind? I like watching you play and cheering for you," Traci said. "You're really good!"

Keith felt that everyone was ganging up on him. He held up a hand like a crossing guard stopping traffic. "Listen up, all of you. I don't want to play football. And I'm not going to play football. Okay? Understand? End of discussion."

He wheeled and walked quickly out of the room.

3

When Keith woke up the next morning, he looked out the window and saw that it was a beautiful, sunny day. He felt great . . . until he remembered what had gone down the previous evening. Then he felt lousy again.

If only he had held on to that pass, Keith thought, his life would be totally different now. Or if he hadn't played football last season . . . or if he'd been an interior lineman, like Cody. Linemen don't get the spotlight. They miss out on the glory, but they also miss out on the humiliation.

Mr. Stedman had already left for work when Keith walked into the kitchen. Neither his mother nor his sister were anywhere to be seen. He poured some orange juice, fixed himself a bowl of cereal,

16

and sat down. After drinking the juice, he stared at the cereal for a while and shoved it away.

He'd always had a healthy appetite, unless he was sick. Until now, at least. He was about to pour the cereal into the disposal when the phone rang. It was Heck.

"How are you doing?" Heck asked. Keith thought his friend sounded a little cautious, like he was choosing his words carefully, not wanting to have any problems.

"Good. What's up?"

"Nothing much," Heck replied. "I was just thinking, it's a nice day, you want to go down to the pool and hang out for a while?"

Keith's first impulse was to turn the idea down, but then he thought, *Why not?* He didn't want to become a total hermit, did he? And Heck was his buddy, right?

"Yeah, sounds good. I'll leave a note saying where I'm going and ride my bike over to your place."

"Cool," Heck said. "See you soon."

Keith scribbled a note for his mom and left it on the hall table. He put on a bathing suit and a T-shirt, grabbed a towel and a change of clothes, and stuffed them in his backpack. Then he rolled his bike out of the garage, hopped on, and pedaled slowly down the street. Heck lived just a few minutes away, and the town's pool and recreation area were also close by. He hoped the subject of football wouldn't come up today, but he had a feeling that it probably would. Heck could be stubborn and he wanted Keith to play with the Bucks.

Well, Keith could be stubborn, too. He wasn't going to change his mind.

Heck was waiting with his bike when Keith rolled into the Szymanskis' driveway. Heck shrugged himself into his backpack and the two friends started toward the park, where the town had a large pool and a field that was used for various sports and events.

"So," Heck said after a few minutes of silence. "How you doing?"

"Okay, I guess," Keith answered.

There was another silence, which Heck broke again.

"I was wondering, who's this guy, uh, Murple, Mertz . . . I can't remember the name."

18

"Huh?" Keith blinked, not sure what Heck was talking about.

"That guy you mentioned last night, the old ballplayer who made the mistake."

Keith realized what Heck meant. "His name was Fred Merkle. He played for the New York Giants baseball team, like, ninety years ago. My dad read about this stuff, he told me.

"Anyway, Merkle was a good baseball player. Well, this one year, I think 1908, the Giants and the Cubs were playing a game. The winner would win the National League and play in the World Series. The score was tied in the ninth inning and the Giants had runners on first and third. Merkle was the runner on first. A base hit would win the game.

"The next guy up hit a single and the guy from third scored. The game was over, the Giants had won. Merkle ran off the field.

"Only he hadn't run all the way to second base. He figured the game was over. That's what usually happened in those days. Except a Cub player yelled that Merkle hadn't reached second base, grabbed the ball, and stepped on second. The umpire said Merkle was out and the run didn't count. They had to replay the game, and this time the Cubs won. They went to the Series instead of the Giants. So, for the rest of his life, Merkle was called 'Bonehead.' He played for a long time, and was good, too. But all the fans remembered was that one mistake. Merkle said that when he died, they'd probably carve 'Bonehead' on his grave. One mistake. That was all it took."

"Huh," said Heck. "I see. Yeah, that was a bad deal he got. But that was Major League baseball. Everybody watches that. I mean, that's not what happened to you, you know?"

Keith sighed. He had known that it would come up again. "Look," he said. "You don't get it. It didn't happen to *you*. It wasn't a picture of *you* lying there on the ground in the newspaper. It was *me*."

"Well, yeah, sure," said Heck, "but still, people have mostly forgotten about it by now. If you'd just come back and play, you'd —"

"*No*. I'm not going to play. I told you that yesterday, and you're not going to change my mind, so I wish you'd drop it. I know you think you're right and I'm wrong, but I don't want to talk about it anymore."

"Sure, I understand . . . but —"

"No, buts!" Keith brought his bike to a screeching stop. "If you don't cut it out, I'm going to turn around and go home. You have to promise. Yes or no?"

Heck braked to a stop and looked at the ground. "I was just —"

"*Yes or no?*"

Heck took a deep breath and nodded. "Okay, yes. You win."

The boys made the rest of the trip in silence.

At the pool, Keith spotted a few of the other Bucks in the shallow end of the pool. One was Cody Aarons, who held a large beach ball over his head while a few other boys tried to knock it loose. For a moment he wondered whether coming to the pool had been a good idea, but before he could decide, Cody spotted him and let out a happy yell.

"*YO! Keith, my man!* Hey, Heck! Hey, come on in, dudes!"

Keith waved and smiled. "Be right there!" He walked his bike to where he could chain it up and went with Heck to the locker room to stow his gear.

While he got his towel out, he tried to think positively. *These guys are my friends, my teammates. They're on my side. Definitely. Absolutely. For sure.*

But he was having a hard time persuading himself of that.

Once he'd changed, Keith ran over to the pool and jumped in. Grinning, Cody left his other friends, wrapped Keith in a bear hug, lifted him up, and dropped him into the water with a splash.

"Lookin' good, dude! Hey, how come you missed the meeting yesterday? You're going to make it to practice, right? We're going to be tough this year."

Keith shook his head. "I won't be there, Code."

The big lineman stared at Keith, and then shook his head from side to side. "Guess I have water in my ears and didn't hear right. It sounded like you said you weren't coming out. But that can't be right."

"Your ears are working fine," replied Keith. "You heard what I said."

Cody looked at Keith as though the other boy were speaking some strange, unknown language. "But . . . how come? Why —"

Cody's eyes shifted away from Keith over his

shoulder. Keith looked around and saw Heck, who had evidently signaled to Cody to stop asking questions.

"Um . . . sorry to hear it," Cody mumbled. "But if that's what you . . . later."

He rejoined the first group of boys. Keith saw him talking to them quietly, after which a few of them looked in his direction. Keith turned to Heck, who had joined him in the pool. "Maybe I should've stayed home today."

Heck laughed. "You planning on becoming a hermit for the rest of your life? Listen, you don't want to play football? Okay, then don't, it's your choice. But to run and hide just because someone *might* make some dumb remark about you, that's a bad idea, period. Lighten up!"

Keith smiled gratefully at his friend. "You're right. I'm letting this thing get to me way too much."

"Now you're making sense!" Heck said. "Come on, those guys are having fun!"

They swam over to Cody and his group, who were tossing the huge beach ball back and forth. Cody saw Keith coming and threw the ball high in the air in his direction.

As Keith reached for it, he heard one of the others say, "Think you can hang on to *this* one, Keith?"

Somebody else snickered. Keith caught the ball, fired it back hard toward the others, and turned away, sure everyone in the pool had heard the nasty crack and was laughing at him.

Heck caught up to him and grabbed his arm. "Come on, man, it was a *joke*. Just a dumb joke. The guy didn't mean anything by it. Chill out and come over."

But Keith shook his head. "You go on. I don't feel like it right now."

He climbed slowly out of the pool and sat on a folding chair under a canvas umbrella. He stared at the ground, feeling hurt and angry.

Would he ever put this behind him?

4

That evening, Keith sat by himself in his backyard, looking through a sports magazine but not paying much attention to it, when he heard his name called and looked up.

Heck and Cody peered cautiously out the back door, as if they weren't at all sure what kind of reception they could expect.

"Okay if we sit down?" Cody asked.

Keith shrugged. "Suit yourselves."

Once they were seated, Cody glanced at Heck and cleared his throat. "I, uh, I just wanted to say, that guy who made the stupid remark at the pool today . . . he isn't one of the Bucks."

"Right," Heck said. "He was just a creep who happened to be hanging out and thought he was being funny."

"He knows different now," Cody snapped, frowning darkly. "I told him to watch his mouth from now on, or he'd be sorry."

Keith managed a weak smile. "Thanks. I appreciate what you're saying, but you didn't really have to do that."

"Yeah, I know I didn't *have* to," said Cody, hitching his chair closer to Keith. "I *wanted* to. I mean, we're friends, right? And the guy was dissing you, and I didn't like it."

Keith nodded. "Well, thanks for standing up for me. I really mean it. But let's face it. The guy was only saying what a lot of kids have been thinking."

Cody rolled his eyes. "But the thing is, that isn't true!"

"Cody's right," Heck said. "For sure, nobody who ever played a sport would give you grief for what happened in that game. We all know that anyone can make a mistake. It could have been one of us."

Cody laughed. "Probably *will* be one of us next time. And there's going to be a next time."

"You shouldn't let someone like that dude at the pool get to you, that's the main thing we want to tell you." Heck leaned forward and stared hard at Keith. "Your real friends know better. It's important that you understand how we feel."

"I know how you two feel," replied Keith. "And I think probably a lot of the other guys on the team feel the same way — not all of them, but a lot. But if I were to play and drop another pass or two, well . . . they'd start changing their minds."

"That doesn't make sense," Heck protested. "You aren't going to start dropping passes. So why worry about it?"

"See, that's the thing." Keith shook his head. "I don't know what I'd do. I think I'd start thinking about messing up the second my number is called. And the more I think about it, the more likely I am to blow it again."

Heck and Cody looked at each other, clearly exasperated. "But you're not making any — Oh, hi, Mr. Stedman."

Keith's father stepped out into the yard. "Hi, boys. Nice night."

"For sure," Heck answered.

"Mr. Stedman," Heck said, "maybe you can help us out here."

Mr. Stedman squatted next to his son on the terrace. "If I can, I will. What's up?"

"We're trying to talk Keith into changing his mind about football," explained Cody. "We could definitely use him this season, and we know he'd be a game-breaker for us."

"I see," said Keith's father, turning to study his son's expression. "But I don't see how I can help you with this."

Heck cleared his throat and thought carefully before speaking. "The thing is, I mean, *you'd* like to see Keith play ball with us this season, wouldn't you? Don't you think he's making a mistake, staying away?"

Mr. Stedman stood up, wincing. "Stiff knee," he said. "Guess I'm getting a little old. Boys, I'm sorry, but I don't think I can help you here. Whether Keith plays football or not is up to him, and I have nothing to say about it."

Cody blurted, "But if you —"

Mr. Stedman held up a hand as if he were stopping traffic at a crossing. "I meant that. It's not my place to give an opinion or say anything about this matter unless Keith asks me to say something. Otherwise, I'm keeping my mouth shut."

He looked down at his son. "Want me to say anything?"

"No, I guess not," replied the boy. "Except . . . well, except, thanks. For not butting in, I mean."

Mr. Stedman patted his son's shoulder. "That's all right. Guys, I'll see you later. And I'm sorry I couldn't help, but it isn't my place to get involved here."

He went back inside.

The three boys sat silently for a minute. Keith didn't know what to say and neither, apparently, did his friends.

Finally, Heck spoke. "I guess Cody and I sort of hoped you'd change your mind, but . . . okay, if you won't, you won't."

"I just don't think I want to do it this year," Keith said. "But we're still friends, right?"

"Sure," Heck said, but Keith didn't think he sounded very enthusiastic about it. "It's just we won't be seeing that much of you once practice starts."

"Yeah, I know," Keith agreed, not happy with that notion.

"Well, maybe we could watch some videos this weekend or go to a movie," suggested Heck.

"Sure, that'd be cool," Keith said.

Cody stood up, looking unhappy. "I have to go home. You coming, Heck?"

Heck shook his head. "Go ahead, I'll see you tomorrow, all right?"

"Yeah, sure." Cody kicked the ground and stood there, looking from Heck to Keith. "Anyway . . . later, guys."

Keith watched Cody walk out of the yard and turned to Heck. "I know you think I'm being a total jerk —"

"No, you don't," Heck cut in.

Keith was startled. "Huh?"

"You *don't* know what I think," Heck said calmly. "So don't say you do. I don't think you're being a total jerk at all. But, if we're really going to talk about this, I'll tell you what I *do* think."

Keith shrugged. "Go ahead."

"I think you feel like it was all your fault that we lost that game, and that's not true. Billy overthrew a pass in the first half when you were totally open and if you'd caught it we would have had six points more than we did.

"Cody missed a block that let a guy get through and throw me for a loss. If we'd gotten a first down there we might have scored a touchdown. The tight end didn't make a move toward the sideline when he was supposed to and if he had, maybe we'd have scored on that series. The —"

"Okay, okay, I see what you're saying," Keith said impatiently. "But we *still* would have won the game if I had caught that last pass . . . which I should have and didn't."

Heck sighed and said, "Wow. You really have a high opinion of yourself, don't you?"

Stung, Keith snapped, "What is that supposed to mean? What are you talking about?"

"Anyone else can make a mistake and it's no big deal, but when *you* make one, it's like, '*Stop the presses! The great Keith Stedman messed up!*' The rest of us guys are allowed to mess up, but not Keith Stedman!"

"Very funny!" Keith yelled.

"No, it's not funny — it's sad," Heck said. "You're

the one who's giving yourself a hard time. If you'd just let it go, so would everyone else. But if you can't, you're better off staying out of sports. You'll just drive yourself crazy, and take your friends along for the ride."

He jumped up and walked quickly away. Keith got to his feet and noticed that his little sister was standing there, looking upset. How much had she heard and understood?

He smiled, trying to look as if everything was cool. "Hey, Trace, what's up?"

She didn't say a word, but it seemed like she might be about to cry.

"Trace? What's the matter? Come on, you can tell me, what is it?"

Very softly, almost too softly for him to hear, she said, "You'll be mad at me."

"No, I won't. Come on, Trace, I promise I won't get mad. If there's something wrong, tell me. Please?"

"Aren't you going to play football anymore? Ever?"

Keith didn't know what to say.

"I'm not going to play for a while, anyway. I don't know about 'ever.' But not right now. Did you hear what Heck and I were talking about out here?"

She nodded. "Uh-huh. You were having an argument."

"Well, I wouldn't call it an *argument* exactly, Trace. . . ."

"And you said you didn't want to play football and I felt sad."

Keith walked over and kneeled down facing the young girl. "Why does my not playing football make you sad?"

"Because I liked to go and see you play and now I won't be able to. And the last thing I'll remember about you playing football will be you dropping that ball and lying there on the ground. If you played some more, you'd do good things and I'd have those to remember instead of that. That's why I feel sad."

She went into the house, leaving Keith standing there by himself, thinking hard about what she'd said.

5

The following day was Sunday, and Mr. Stedman was trimming a hedge when Keith walked outside and stood watching him.

"Hey, Slugger," said Keith's father, not looking up. "You slept late this morning, huh?"

"Yeah . . . well, no. I was sort of lying there, thinking. Do you have time to talk?"

Mr. Stedman stopped clipping and stretched. "I could use a break, anyway. Want some lemonade? There's a fresh pitcher in the refrigerator."

"No, I'm okay. I can get you some if you want," Keith offered.

"I can hold out awhile. Come on, sit here." Mr. Stedman led the way and sat on the front-porch steps. "Does this have to do with the conversation with Heck and Cody?"

"Yeah." Keith sat with his father. "Heck's mad because I won't play with the Bucks."

"Is that right? Hmmm . . . somehow, that doesn't sound like the Heck I know."

"Well, he sure sounded mad when he stomped out of here. And he said that I think a lot of myself, too. That's not fair."

"How did he mean that? I mean, what do you think he meant? That you're always bragging about how good you are?"

Keith shook his head. "No, he knows that I don't do that stuff."

"What, then?"

"Well . . ." Keith thought back. "He said that I think it's okay for other players to mess up, but when *I* do it, it's bad."

"Uh-huh."

"That's wrong! And he ought to know it! I'm not a selfish player!"

"I don't think that's what Heck meant."

"Well, what, then?"

Mr. Stedman turned to face his son. "It sounds like he thinks you expect too much of yourself, more than you expect of other players. It's like you have a higher standard for your playing than for the rest of the team's. That's not selfishness, but it can be a problem for you."

"A problem?" Keith looked skeptical. "How can wanting to play well be a problem?"

Keith's father sighed. "It's not wanting to play well, it's. . . . Before I say any more, I want one thing clear. Whether you play football or not is *your* decision to make, and I'm going to try not to push you one way or the other. That's not my place. I hope that's understood."

"Sure."

"All right, then." Mr. Stedman stood up. "All athletes, no matter what level they're playing at, no matter how good they are, will make mistakes. People make mistakes, that's human nature. Sometimes you'll do it at an especially bad time, when it'll have serious consequences, or when you're in the public eye and everyone sees you.

"Now, it seems to me that what you have to do then is move on. You can learn from it, but you shouldn't dwell on it. Once it's done, you have to leave it behind you. And, even more important, you can't spend your life looking to avoid all the situations where you might mess up. If you do that, you're likely to end up sitting there and doing nothing at all, or nothing that really matters. You'll always be afraid, you'll forever be saying, 'What if?' That's no way to live. You're thirteen, and you have your life ahead of you. I would hate to see you let this one incident have such a huge effect on you.

"But, like I said before, what you choose to do is up to you. Just know that, whatever you decide, Mom and I will always be here for you. But you already know that."

Keith nodded, grateful for what his dad had said. "Yeah, sure I do. And thanks. I'll think it over."

"Good." Mr. Stedman looked up and studied the sky. "Know what? It's too beautiful a day to spend working on the yard. Want to toss a football around for a while?"

"Yeah, sure!" said Keith.

"Hang on a minute and I'll get the ball."

Keith sat and thought about what his dad had told him. Maybe, he thought, he'd been thinking too long and hard about that game. Maybe he ought to try to give it a rest . . . maybe . . .

"Sorry it took me so long," said Mr. Stedman as he returned with the football. "Ready?"

Keith admitted to himself that he felt nervous as he walked into the yard. It would be the first time anyone would have thrown him a ball since . . . since that day last fall.

His father threw a lazy, soft pass and Keith felt his whole body get tense as he reached for it . . . and bobbled it on his fingertips, before getting it under control and hanging on. He flipped the ball back to Mr. Stedman, who threw it back again, slightly harder and on a flatter line.

After a few more catches and throws, Keith was feeling more at ease. His father waved at him to cut across the yard, then fired a bullet that Keith snared easily.

"Nice! You know," said Mr. Stedman, "you're looking like you did last season. Really."

Keith smiled, but said, "Sure. When there's no one looking and it doesn't matter, I'm a superstar."

"Maybe you'd look this good even with a bunch of fans whooping and hollering in the bleachers," said his father, cocking his arm to throw again. "Hi, Heck."

Keith turned to see Heck in the driveway, dismounting from his bike.

"Hey, Mr. Stedman," said the other boy. He looked at his friend and nodded casually. "Hey, Keith."

Mr. Stedman tossed another pass to his son, overthrowing it slightly and forcing Keith to lunge for the ball. Keith grabbed it and hung on.

"Looking good," Heck said, clapping. "Is it okay if I get in on this?"

Keith hesitated. Mr. Stedman said nothing and kept his expression neutral. "Sure," Keith said. "Why not?"

He flipped the ball to Heck, who threw it to Keith's father. Within a few minutes, the three were tossing the ball around just as they had done many times over the years. And Keith was surprised that it was normal and natural. A little later, Mr. Stedman excused himself and went inside, while the boys kept going.

At one point, Heck's throw to Keith was low and to one side. Without stopping to think, Keith dived and made a shoestring catch just before he hit the ground.

He got up and brushed dirt off his pants. "Did you do that on purpose?" he demanded, staring hard at Heck.

"No way! The ball just slipped. I'm a running back, not a quarterback, remember?" Heck looked convincing, Keith thought.

"But," Heck added a moment later, "I have to say, you still have good hands, buddy."

Keith smiled. Heck was right about that.

"Listen, if we went to the park, we could air it out more," suggested Heck. "What do you say?"

Keith liked the idea. "Let me just tell Dad where we're going," he said, running to the front door and calling his father.

When Mr. Stedman appeared, Keith said, "We're going to the park for a while."

"Fine. Have fun," his father replied.

Keith was turning to go when a thought struck him. He turned back. "Did you call Heck up and ask him to come over when you went to get the football?"

Mr. Stedman grinned. "You caught me. Are you mad at me?"

Keith tried to keep his face straight, but he couldn't help smiling back. "Nope. Thanks."

"See you later," said his father, patting Keith on the arm.

As the boys biked to the park, Heck said, "Listen, about yesterday. . . . I shot off my mouth too much."

"That's okay," answered Keith. "I thought about what you said, and you probably had a point. Anyway, no hard feelings."

At the park, Keith and Heck threw longer passes and ran patterns. Keith had just made an over-the-shoulder catch running flat out when he heard someone call, "Awesome play!"

He discovered Cody watching from the edge of the grass. "Hey!" Keith called. "Been there long?"

"Just a few minutes. Long enough to see that you look good. We could sure use you this year. I don't want to push it or anything, but . . . is there any chance you might change your mind and show up tomorrow?"

Keith looked from Cody to Heck and back, and said nothing.

"If you don't want to, then that's that," Cody added. "But, is there any chance?"

After chewing on his lower lip a moment, Keith said, "Maybe."

41

The boys played for a while longer, then split for lunch. Keith helped his dad around the yard the rest of the afternoon. His father didn't say a word about football, but it was all Keith thought about.

That night, at dinner, Keith made an announcement.

"I changed my mind about football. I'm going to practice tomorrow — if Coach Bodie is willing to let me play."

"*Yay!*" shrieked Traci, clapping her hands.

"I imagine the coach will be happy to have you there," Mr. Stedman said.

"Of course he will," Mrs. Stedman agreed.

"By the way, what made you decide to go out, after all?" Keith's father asked.

Keith swallowed the piece of steak he'd been chewing. "I thought about what you said yesterday, and you were right. About not being afraid all the time, I mean. I don't want to be afraid of messing up all the time. If it happens, it happens, but I'm going to give it my best shot."

He grinned at Traci.

"I thought about what you said, too, you know, how you didn't want your last football memory of me to be me lying facedown on the dirt? I decided I didn't want other people to remember me for that, either."

"Now you're making sense," said Mr. Stedman.

Keith frowned. "I thought you weren't going to influence my decision."

"I didn't. I waited until you made up your own mind, and now I'm telling you I think you're doing the right thing."

"Huh," Keith muttered. "What if I'd said that I still didn't want to play?"

"In that case," said Mr. Stedman, "I still would have said you were doing the right thing. But I would have realized that maybe you were a different kind of boy from what I believed you were."

Keith decided to take it as a compliment.

6

The next afternoon, Keith and Heck walked onto the field where the Bucks were having their first practice of the season. Now that he had decided to come out for the team after all, Keith was feeling a mixture of eagerness and tension. He wanted to get started and was remembering how much fun football could be, but he was worried about what Coach Bodie's attitude would be and how the rest of the team would feel.

Would the coach be cool toward him because of his earlier unwillingness to play? Would the other Bucks welcome him back, as Heck had assured him they would? Was it possible that they might not be as happy to see him as Heck thought?

Well, he'd find out soon enough, now that he was here. On the field, Keith saw several players already present, wearing helmets and pads. A few were pulling footballs out of canvas bags, while others stretched and warmed up. It was Cody who was the first to spot Keith and Heck. His face broke into a broad grin, and he yelled, "Yo, guys, look who's here!"

It seemed to Keith that several Bucks looked surprised to see him there, but he couldn't read their facial expressions behind the helmets and face masks, so he had no way to know whether it was a pleasant or unpleasant surprise. He would have to wait and see.

It was clear that Cody was delighted. He raced up to Keith, wrapped his arms around him, and lifted him in the air.

"I *knew* it! I *knew* you'd be here! *All right!* Yo, Coach, hey, look who's here!"

Coach Bodie, who had been writing something on a clipboard, looked up and saw Keith. He smiled and walked over.

"Keith! I didn't expect to see you with us today. Does this mean that you want to play, after all? I hadn't heard anything about it."

Keith suddenly felt tongue-tied. He should have

called the coach last night! It was really stupid, just showing up like this when he had said that he wasn't going to play. Now Coach Bodie must think he was a total idiot, walking on the field as if there had never been any question about it.

"I, uh, no, I guess I should have let you know, but . . . the truth is, I only decided I wanted to play last night and . . . I guess I wasn't thinking. I mean, I don't know whether you even want me now, and if you don't, it's my fault for not being, for not —"

"Whoa, settle down," said the coach. "Of course I'm happy to see you here, and I was hoping you'd think better about quitting. I think we can have ourselves a great season, and you can be a big part of it. We're going to get started in a few minutes, so if you want, you can get reacquainted with some of the others and get loose."

Coach Bodie walked off just as Billy Brundage, last year's starting quarterback, and probably this year's, too, came up and exchanged hand slaps with Keith and Heck. "Hey, great to see you. When you weren't at the meeting last week, I was afraid you weren't coming out this year. We're going to have a great season, I can feel it!"

Several other Bucks who Keith knew swarmed around and greeted him happily. Heck poked an elbow into his friend's side. "What did I tell you? They're happy to see you!"

But Keith noticed that a few players had not come over. One he recognized right away: Larry Vincent, a tall, thin wide receiver who had played behind him the previous year, who had had problems with his coordination. Larry had probably figured to be a starter if Keith was out of the picture, and might not have been thrilled to see him show up today. Larry was talking to a boy Keith didn't recognize. He turned to Heck.

"Who's the dude with Larry Vincent?"

Heck shrugged. "New guy in town. I can't remember his name, but I think his family moved in next to Larry's."

"Come on, I want to introduce myself."

Keith and Heck walked over to the two boys, who watched them approach, showing neither pleasure nor hostility.

"Hey, Larry," said Keith. "Good to see you." He turned to the other boy. "I'm Keith Stedman."

"Jason Cole," said the new boy, who had a pale,

freckled face and large hands with long fingers. "How you doing?"

"Hey, Keith," said Larry. "Heck, how's it going?"

"Pretty good," Heck said. "Jason, I'm Heck Szymanski. Good to meet you."

"Hi, Heck," said Jason. Then he turned his attention back to Keith, staring at him with obvious curiosity. Keith was sure that Larry had been telling Jason about the Dropped Pass.

Well, okay, Keith thought. *I did drop the pass. Like Dad said, I can't focus on that, even if someone else wants to.* "Jason, what position do you play?"

"I was the quarterback on the team where I used to live," said Jason, grinning, "and Larry says your other quarterback is too old for this league, so maybe I can replace him. If not, well, I could be a runner or a flanker or something."

Keith nodded. "Well, Larry's right, the guy who used to back Billy up isn't playing with the Bucks this year."

"Good to have you with us," Heck said, reaching out for a hand slap, which Jason gave him.

"Thanks," replied Jason. "I heard you were good last year."

"Yeah," said Larry. "We *almost* had an undefeated season."

Before Keith could decide whether Larry meant that as a dig, the coach blew his whistle. "Okay, let's group up over here," Coach Bodie called out, clapping his hands. He carried his clipboard under one arm.

"Great!" the coach exclaimed, looking at the group of boys. "Good to see that so many of last season's team is here again. We had a lot of success last year, and there's no reason why we can't do it again — if we do our work and think and play as a *team*.

"Those of you who have worked with me before know what I expect from you. For those who haven't, it's pretty simple. I expect everyone to give his best effort at all times, to be sportsmanlike, and keep his head in the game. I know that people will make *physical* mistakes — trip, drop a ball, whatever — and I don't have a problem with that, unless a player makes a habit of it.

"But *mental* mistakes are another matter. If you forget what down it is, or miss a blocking assignment, or run the wrong pass route, then you're probably not concentrating on the job at hand . . .

and that is the kind of foul-up that I don't have much patience with.

"Okay. We only have two weeks before our first game, so we've got our work cut out for us. We'll start out today with a little warm-up, and then we'll break into two groups and work on our offense. I'll work with the backs and receivers, while my assistant, Mack, works with the linemen on blocking."

Mack, a powerfully built man whose cut-off sweatshirt showed off his muscular arms, had been a star tackle on his college team. He smiled and nodded when his name was mentioned.

The warm-up was a short workout with light calisthenics. Coach Bodie didn't believe in a lot of pushups, situps, and stuff like that, although he had no problem if players wanted to do that on their own. But he liked his team to work on their stamina and wind, and ended each practice with a run.

When the backs and receivers went to work, the quarterbacks, including Billy and Jason, would give a receiver or back a pattern to run (with any necessary explanation provided by the coach), and then throw a pass.

At first, the coach assigned Larry to work with Jason rather than Billy, the probable starting quarterback. Keith thought Larry was ready to complain, but stopped at the last moment, since he would have annoyed both Coach Bodie and Jason.

Keith, Heck, and Billy watched as Jason sent Larry out on the first pattern of the day. Larry made an inside fake and cut sharply toward the sideline. Jason's pass was slightly wide, but Larry made a nice lunging catch.

"He's faster than last year," Heck observed.

"Yeah, and he didn't get his feet all tangled up like he used to," commented Billy. Keith kept silent for the moment. But it appeared to him, too, that Larry was looking better than he had the previous year.

When Keith came up to the line for a pass from Billy, the quarterback told him to run a deep hook; he was to start downfield fast, stop short, and make a tight turn inside. The pass, if thrown correctly, would be there for him once he had hooked.

Keith made his fifteen-yard downfield run, put on the brakes, and turned to his right, but the pass was off target, reaching him at ankle level. The best Keith could do was to get one hand on the ball, which bounced and rolled on the ground.

As Keith trotted after the loose ball, he heard snickering coming from the group. He felt a surge of frustration. The pass had been poorly thrown and impossible to catch. He angrily scooped up the ball and started back with it.

"Sorry! My fault!" Billy called, and Keith put on what he hoped would be a convincing smile. But he saw Larry whispering something to Jason, who smiled and nodded.

A few minutes later, Billy sent Keith deep and tossed him a slightly wobbly, underthrown pass that Keith did well to reach back and pull in with one hand.

"All right!" Heck yelled, and Billy clapped his hands. Keith noticed that even the coach, who did not give out praise easily, nodded and seemed pleased. He felt a little better. But, at the same time, Keith realized that Larry was far from the awkward, uncoordinated athlete he had been a year earlier. He was looking good, running tight patterns and hanging on to every ball that came near enough.

Larry was good. Possibly, he might be as good as Keith himself.

His preoccupation with the idea that Larry was now a serious rival for the starting position must have taken Keith's mind off the practice for a moment, because a little while later, he mistakenly cut to the middle while Billy threw a pass toward the sideline.

Disgusted with himself, he kicked at the dirt before looking up to see Coach Bodie frowning at him.

"Sorry!" he called out. "I wasn't thinking. It won't happen again!"

As he went to get the ball, Keith heard Billy call out some encouragement. But he was still annoyed at his blunder, and thought to himself that, this year, he was in for a real battle, and he couldn't afford to mess up like he had just done.

Or else he might find himself on the sideline a lot more than he wanted, once the games began.

7

"You looked good yesterday," Heck said, as he and Keith headed for the second day of practice. Cody was with them.

"And the whole team was glad to see that you decided to come back," said Cody, to which Heck nodded in agreement.

Keith wasn't so sure. "Thanks, guys. I guess I did all right, and I know you two are happy that I'm playing, and that some others are, too. But, 'the whole team'? I don't *think* so. Not everyone."

Cody looked startled. "Huh? What are you talking about? Who wasn't glad?"

"Larry Vincent didn't look overjoyed, for one," Keith pointed out.

Cody's face took on a look of disgust. "Oh, *him*. Well, so what? The dude is a loser. Don't pay any attention to him, and don't worry about anything he has to say, either."

"What do you mean?" demanded Keith. "What is Larry saying?"

Before Cody could answer, Heck said, "*Cody* . . . cool it, would you?"

"No, really," Keith said. "I want to know. Come on, Cody, what is Larry saying? Don't worry — I'm not going to start a fight with him or anything."

Cody looked unhappily at Heck before answering. "Oh, just stupid stuff about the game last year, and what happened . . . you know, really dumb stuff."

Keith nodded. "How I cost us the unbeaten season and the championship, *that* kind of stuff?"

"Which we all know is total garbage," Cody said quickly. "Like I said, nothing for you to pay attention to or worry about."

"Absolutely," Heck agreed. "The rest of the team knows that without you we probably never would have had a shot at an unbeaten season. Larry's just jealous, that's all."

"Sure," Cody said as they reached the practice area. "Because Larry knows he can't compete with you — that you'll be our top receiver again this year, and he'll spend a lot of time on the bench."

"Hey, guys," said Keith, "I know you two are on my side all the way, but you saw the practice yesterday. Heck, you know that Larry is a lot better than he was a year ago. He's going to be a player this season. He'll make a contribution.

"And as far as I'm concerned, that's cool. We can use another good downfield threat. I don't know much about what kind of guy Larry is, but he's improved a lot."

"True," admitted Heck, "but he better not badmouth you. For one thing, if Coach hears him doing that, the least that'll happen is that Larry will get a major chewing out."

"He'll get worse from me, if *I* hear any more out of him," growled Cody.

Keith put a hand on Cody's shoulder. "Listen, I know you're trying to help me, but if you get into it with Larry over this, you won't be helping me *or* the team. And you might be the one to get chewed out."

"Keith's right," Heck said. "Don't add to the problem — if there *is* a problem. Okay, Code?"

The husky lineman said, "Yeah, I know, you're

right. But it gets me hot when this dude talks about Keith behind his back, that's all."

"I can handle it, don't worry," Keith insisted.

As they walked onto the field, Keith saw that the coach was talking to a man he didn't recognize. The man seemed unhappy, and from Coach Bodie's expression, the conversation appeared to be an argument. Finally, the strange man threw his hands in the air and walked away, looking like he hadn't heard anything to please him.

"Who is that?" Keith asked.

Heck shook his head. "Never saw him before."

Cody scowled. "That's Larry Vincent's dad. He dropped Larry off at practice yesterday."

"What's his problem?" Heck wondered.

"Beats me," Keith said, suspecting that he himself might have been the subject of the discussion, argument, or whatever it was.

Shortly afterward, the coach called the team together. "There's a point I wanted to mention to everybody before we go to work. I spoke about it yesterday but I'm going to repeat myself, because I don't want anyone to forget it or misunderstand me on this subject.

"Everyone makes mistakes in sports. Pros, even all-time greats, do it. So I figure that you're likely to make some, too, at one time or another. And that's to be expected. When you make a *physical* mistake — like dropping a ball — well, that's just one of those things, and there's no blame attached. *None*. I want each and every one of you to get that clear.

"The kind of mistake that bothers me is the *mental* kind — the kind that shows that you're not thinking, or that you're not thinking like a team player. When that happens, the person responsible is going to hear from me. Count on it. Now, let's get to work."

Once again, the backs and receivers stayed in one group with Coach Bodie while the interior linemen went with Mack. As they grouped up, Heck nudged Keith. "What was *that* about, do you think?"

Keith shrugged. "Who knows?"

But he thought that it might have been aimed at Larry and his father . . . and at him. He figured — and hoped — that the coach was reassuring him and warning Larry.

In today's drill, Coach Bodie had one receiver run a pattern while another receiver played defense and covered him. Jason was to throw to Keith with Larry defending, while Keith had to try to stop Larry from catching passes from Billy.

On Larry's first effort to get clear, he made a downfield run and an obvious fake to the outside, which Keith ignored. When Larry cut across the field, Keith was with him step for step, and even though Billy's pass was accurate, Keith got a hand in to deflect it.

"Good reaction, Keith!" the coach called out. "Larry, watch your fakes. You need to put more movement into them. You can't just bob your head like that."

Larry nodded, looking unhappy. Keith tapped his shoulder. "I was watching your belt buckle, not your head. That's why I didn't buy your outside move."

Larry mumbled something that might have been thanks, but Keith couldn't understand him.

When Keith went down and out for a pass from Jason, he used a stutter-step that froze Larry just long enough for Keith to get free. Jason's pass, how-ever, was thrown slightly behind Keith, who couldn't control it to make the catch. As he came back to the group, he noticed Larry whispering to Jason, who smothered a laugh.

Knowing that the pass had been poorly thrown, Keith was irritated. He couldn't help wondering if Larry had tried to put the blame for the missed catch on Keith. If so, Jason seemed only too happy to believe that the fault had been with the receiver and not the passer. But maybe he was all wrong, and in any case, Keith didn't think that he should say anything. He was determined to let his play speak for him.

As the drill went on, Keith saw that Larry was a step faster than he was, but he made up for it with better coordination and moves than Larry. Though Larry had improved from the previous year, he still couldn't control his lanky legs that well. Still, Keith thought the two of them were pretty evenly matched.

Unfortunately, Jason was proving to be a less accurate passer than Billy, sometimes overthrowing and sometimes throwing wide. As a result, Keith caught fewer balls. Keith assumed Coach Bodie would see that the missed passes were largely due to Jason's arm, rather than his hands.

But the coach didn't have much to say to Jason, so Keith couldn't be certain that he was correct. Little by little, Keith began to simmer, but said nothing and did nothing to show it. He noticed that Heck was trying to encourage him, smiling and giving him the thumbs-up when Keith made a good move and pointing out when Keith was not at fault on a blown play. Keith felt grateful but continued to steam.

He also noticed Larry taking one or two players aside now and then, especially after Keith had not held on to a pass. Keith became convinced that Larry was trying to promote himself as a better player than Keith.

Were other Bucks in agreement? There was no way to know.

Finally, Keith went long on a deep fly pattern, leaving Larry, who he had faked out with a hip move, trailing by several steps. But he would have needed a stepladder to catch Jason's pass, which sailed a few feet over his head. Keith slowed down and stopped — and was jarred a second later when Larry ran into him from behind.

"Hey!" Keith snapped, rubbing his back where the other boy had slammed him. "Watch it! Didn't you see I had stopped?"

"No, I didn't see you'd stopped!" Larry yelled back. "I figured that you'd keep hustling, like a football player is supposed to. But I guess that's not your style, huh?"

All Keith's anger suddenly came to a boil. A little voice in his brain advised him to cool it, but he couldn't do it.

"'Hustling'?" he shouted. "It's not 'hustling' to chase a pass that's ten feet over your head! It's just dumb. Maybe that's *your* style! That and ramming into someone when his back is turned!"

"I didn't see you!" Larry yelled.

"Yeah, right!" Keith screamed.

By this time the two boys were nose to nose, both yelling, with other players staring. Keith noticed Heck running up and trying to get between them.

"Chill out, guys," he urged. "This is bad news, come on . . ."

"What's happening here?" Coach Bodie suddenly loomed in front of the arguing players, who immediately separated and became quiet.

"I asked what was happening here?" the coach repeated, looking at both boys with a severe expression. "I turn away for a minute and I find two teammates spitting at each other like wildcats! Now what's the deal here?"

Keith took a deep breath. "Sorry, Coach. It's just that he just ran into me hard from behind, and I guess I got shook up."

"Well," said Larry, "he stopped short instead of running out a pattern, and I wasn't expecting it!"

"I *didn't* stop short," Keith came back. "I just —"

The coach cut him off. "*Enough*! That'll do! Both of you, come with me." He looked at the other players, who were watching the action. "The rest of you, take a break."

He led Keith and Larry away until they were out of earshot of the rest of the team. Then he faced them, his arms folded across his chest. "Maybe I didn't make clear to you two this morning the way I feel about mental mistakes. I'm going to try one more time, and I hope you're both paying very close attention this time.

"Mental mistakes show that you aren't thinking *like a team player*. When two teammates fight with each other, they're not thinking like team players. Did you understand me that time?"

"Yeah, but —" Larry started, and Coach Bodie jumped in immediately.

"'Yeah, but . . .' is not the right answer to the

question I asked. One more time: Do you under-stand what I'm telling you?"

"Yes, Coach," Keith said, staring at the ground and feeling very foolish.

"Yes, Coach," Larry echoed.

"That's the right answer." The coach took a deep breath. "Okay. I don't know what started this, and I am not even going to ask. I don't want to get into one of these 'He said this but I said that' situations. You are *teammates* and you have to remember that. If there's a problem between you, work it out. If I have to be brought into it again, neither of you will be happy with the result. Now let's go to work."

Keith couldn't help feeling like he'd been treated unfairly, because he thought Larry was to blame for what had happened. But he decided the smart thing was to get past it.

In the next half hour, Keith made some good plays, including a diving catch that drew praise from the coach and an interception of one of Billy's passes. He felt better afterward.

But he kept spotting Larry having those whis-pered conversations with Jason and other Bucks.

8

The roar was deafening. Keith looked up at grandstands that seemed to rise into the clouds, and every one of the hundreds of thousands of seats was full, and the fans were all yelling at the tops of their lungs.

Billy kept throwing passes to him, and he was always clear . . . and he couldn't hold on to any of them. He dropped one after another and each time there would be a thundering chorus of boos.

Gasping for breath, Keith spotted his family sitting in the front row, looking very sad. His father was shaking his head, and Traci was crying. All of his teammates, even Heck and Cody, kept pointing at him and scowling, while Larry Vincent kept smirking and shouting, "What did I tell you? He's pathetic! He's a loser!"

Coach Bodie called time-out and ran over to him, screaming, "We're going to keep throwing you the ball until you get it right!"

Keith's legs felt like they were made of cement, and he couldn't move. Billy threw another pass, but the ball went way over his head while he just stood there, feeling completely helpless. . . . He was a loser. . . . He was a loser. . . .

Suddenly, Keith woke up. He felt shaky and was sweating heavily. The dial of his bedside clock read 3:30 A.M. He fell back on the pillow and closed his eyes. But the awful nightmare stayed with him and he couldn't get back to sleep for what seemed like hours.

When Keith sat down to have breakfast the next morning — the first day of school — his parents studied him carefully.

"Are you feeling all right, Keith?" his mother asked. "You look like you might be coming down with something."

"No, I'm okay, Mom, really." Keith knew that he must look awful after getting so little sleep the night before, but he didn't want to talk about it with his mom and dad, and certainly not in front of Traci. Although he didn't have much of an appetite, he managed to eat everything on his plate. He hoped that this would reassure his parents.

"Well, I better get ready," he said, getting up. "Big day today."

As he grabbed his backpack and windbreaker, his father followed him toward the front door. "Got a second, Slugger?"

Keith was reluctant to talk to his dad, not wanting to discuss what was on his mind. "I really have to get moving."

"This won't take long, I promise."

Keith couldn't see any way out of it. "Well . . . okay." He sat down on the porch steps, with Mr. Stedman next to him.

"You had some trouble sleeping last night, huh?" said his father.

Keith was surprised. "How'd you know?"

"I'm a light sleeper myself, and I heard you doing some serious tossing and turning. I don't think your mom knew — she could sleep through an artillery battle — but I knew, and I was wondering what was up. Could this have anything to do with football, and what you'd been worrying about?"

Keith was always startled at his father's instinct for what was on his son's mind. He had thought about ducking the question, but decided that maybe it was best to talk about it.

"The thing is . . . ," he started, and then stopped, not sure of *what* the thing was. Then he blurted, "Maybe I was wrong about playing football, after all. I don't know."

Mr. Stedman pursed his lips. "And last night has something to do with what you're thinking?"

"I had this really terrible nightmare about football, and it made me think that maybe Larry Vincent is right. Maybe I'm just going to hurt the team."

"Who is this Larry Vincent, and how do you know what he thinks?"

Keith explained what Larry was doing and what had happened the previous day. "I don't know. . . . It could happen again. . . . I don't know what I'd do if that happened. Maybe I should just quit and stay out."

"I see," Keith's dad said. "Have you considered talking to Larry? Just the two of you, face to face, saying what's on your mind?"

Keith shook his head. "No way, I couldn't do that. I just couldn't."

"All right. Here's my opinion." Mr. Stedman fixed his son with a serious look. "I think you're a fine athlete and that you're more likely to help your team than hurt it. Of course, there are no guarantees. But I wish you'd stick it out, and if your teammates doubt you, you'll convince them by playing your best."

Keith stood up. "I better go, but . . . okay. I won't quit. I guess you're right."

In his heart, Keith wasn't sure at all.

The first morning of school was busy. At the lunch break, Keith headed for the cafeteria feeling hungry. He looked around for Heck, whom he'd promised to meet, and spotted him across the noisy room. Sitting next to him, talking a mile a minute, was Larry. Keith felt a sudden lurch in his stomach and headed toward the table.

Larry saw him coming and said a few more words to Heck, who looked uncomfortable and said nothing in return. Then Larry walked away, carefully avoiding Keith's eyes.

"Hey," said Keith, sitting across from his friend.

"How are you doing?" asked Heck, who seemed nervous.

Keith wasn't interested in small talk. "What did *he* want?"

Heck shrugged and muttered, "Oh, nothing much. Just . . . you know."

"Uh-huh," Keith said. "Nothing much. Just talking about the weather, huh?"

"Well . . ." Heck looked down at his lunch tray.

"Come on, Heck, be straight with me," Keith urged. "What did he want?"

After hesitating a moment, Heck said, "What do you think? He was saying that he should be the go-to guy this season, that you can't be trusted to make the big play. I told him I didn't want to hear that stuff and that you're a great receiver. I said that he had no business talking about you behind your back and that he'd better cut it out."

Keith slumped in his chair, his appetite gone. "I don't know. Maybe he's right."

Heck's jaw dropped open. *"Huh?"*

"Maybe I *would* hurt the team."

Heck's eyes blazed angrily. "Listen up! The only way you'll hurt the Bucks is if you wimp out and quit! I don't believe this! Here's what you better do: You better show up and go all out and make Larry look like a total doofus for putting you down. You're a better receiver than he is, and all you have to do is show it. Coach Bodie will see it, too.

"So . . . you coming to practice this afternoon, or not?" Heck demanded.

Keith sighed. Then he nodded. "I'll be there."

9

The next couple of days went smoothly for Keith, who thought he performed well, on both offense and defense, where he was clearly better than Larry because of his reflexes and coordination. Possibly because of that, or because Heck had warned him, Larry had called off his whispering campaign against Keith — at least for the time being. The coach was satisfied with the team's progress, and Keith relaxed his suspicion.

With a little more than a week left before the first game of the season, Coach Bodie started running intrasquad scrimmages, in which one section of the team defended against the other group. Keith felt good about the fact that he was teamed up with Billy, Heck, and Cody on what looked like the first string . . . until the coach switched people around.

His high point came when Billy tried an end around. He faked a handoff to Heck and pitched the ball to Keith, who was circling around from right end to the left side. Cody pulled out of the line to make a downfield block and Keith sped down the sideline for a big gain, faking Larry out of his socks in the process. Sometimes, life was good.

A few plays later, Billy called the same halfback option play that had been Keith's downfall the previous year. Keith had to go downfield while Billy lateraled to Heck, who would throw a long pass to Keith, now presumably in the clear.

Sure enough, Keith got past Larry and looked back for the pass. But he was shocked to see Heck pump the ball once, tuck it under his arm, and run! He got three yards before three defenders, including Larry, brought him down. Keith ran up to Heck as he got to his feet.

"I was wide open!" he yelled. "Why didn't you pass?"

Heck stared at Keith, startled. "There were guys

in front of me and I couldn't see you. Also, I figured I had more running room than I really did. What's the big deal?"

Keith glared at his friend. "You didn't want to throw me the ball! Admit it!"

"Are you serious?" demanded Heck, getting angry himself. "You ought to know better than that!"

Larry, who had been eagerly following the argument, muttered, "If he *didn't* want to throw the guy the ball, can you blame him?" He spoke loud enough for Keith to hear, but not the coach, who was some distance away.

"Shut your mouth!" Keith yelled. This time, Coach Bodie *did* hear, and blew his whistle. "Keith, get over here!"

Steaming, Keith trotted over to the coach and started to explain what had happened. But the man shook his head.

"I don't want to hear it, son. The thing is, the time has come for you to think about playing ball and stop looking for things to get mad about."

"But —"

Coach Bodie held up a hand. "No 'buts.' I'll talk to Larry and Heck separately, don't you worry. However, what bothers me most here is that you still seem to have a real problem with hurt feelings. It could split the team into opposing sides. I won't let that happen. You're a talented player, and you can make a major contribution to the Bucks, I know that. But the quarreling and the bad feeling can't go on.

"I think you can get past this and get back to what matters out here. At least, I *hope* you can. But for now, I want you to take the rest of the afternoon off and think real hard about whether or not you want to get yourself focused on the team, rather than yourself.

"If you decide you can do it, then we'll see you tomorrow."

10

Keith walked home, getting angrier with every step. Everyone was being unfair, everyone was treating him like he was to blame. Not just Larry, either: the coach, his teammates, even his so-called friend, Heck, had turned against him. And he was also angry with himself. It seemed like he simply couldn't control these outbursts that made him look like an idiot. Why couldn't he just do what his father said, play the game and ignore all the bad stuff?

But he couldn't. If he had only —

"Keith! Hey, *Keith!* Wait up!!"

Turning to see who was calling him, Keith saw Heck running after him and catching up. He turned away and started walking again, faster.

"Keith! Stop!"

When Keith wouldn't stop walking, Heck went around him and stood there, blocking his path.

"Leave me alone," Keith snapped.

"I don't believe this! You really think I turned against you? I've been your best friend for years, and now you think I'm not your friend anymore?"

"I don't want to talk about it," Keith said, feeling torn and foolish.

"Well, I want an answer!" Heck's face was red and his fists were clenched. "We've been buddies all this time, but now you think I'm not your friend anymore. Is that right or wrong?"

Keith realized he was going to have to say something. "I think you decided that Larry was right, that I'm just a choke artist. Okay? You wanted an answer, now you have it."

Heck blinked, opened his mouth, then closed it again. When he spoke, his voice was quiet.

"Okay. If that's how you feel, then fine. I've been on your side all this time. So was everyone else, except Larry. But you know what? If that's how you feel, then I guess I was wrong about you. You're a quitter. You'd rather run away from a problem than

77

do something about it. You want to quit? Okay, then, quit. I'm tired of this. See you around."

He walked past Keith and headed away, not looking back. Keith watched him go, feeling miserable. He'd really blown it now.

That evening, before dinner, Keith went to his father, who was watching TV in the den.

"I've had it with football. I quit. Now everyone hates me, even Heck. I don't think they'd want me back even if I wanted to come. And even Larry's father was working against me, trying to get the coach to play Larry in front of me. It's not fair, and I'm sick of it!"

Mr. Stedman put down his book. "Joe Vincent? You think he's involved? I know Joe, and I have a hard time seeing him doing such a thing. I think you should calm down and give it a rest, and then we can talk —"

"No more talk! I don't want to talk about it. I better go do my homework." Keith headed to his room, where he sulked until it was time to eat.

Traci was too young to understand that Keith's silence at the table meant that he was in a bad mood. She asked, "How is football going?"

Keith dropped his fork and snarled, "Will everybody stop talking to me about *football*? I don't want to say anything about football! Okay?"

Stunned, not knowing what she'd done, Traci began to cry. As soon as he saw tears running down his sister's face, Keith felt like a total jerk. "Trace? Hey, listen, I'm sorry, I didn't mean to yell at you, it's not your fault. I'm just a creep. Okay? Please don't cry."

Traci dried her eyes, and dinner resumed, but nobody looked happy. A few minutes later, Mr. Stedman said, "Keith, after dinner you and I are going to talk. That's an order."

Keith nodded and realized that he'd gone too far. His father was usually an easygoing guy, but now Keith knew that his dad was annoyed.

Once the table was clear, Keith and his father went into the den. "Sit," said Mr. Stedman, pointing to a chair. "I spoke to Joe Vincent after our earlier conversation."

"You *did*? I didn't want —"

"I did what I thought had to be done. I told Joe that there seemed to be a problem between you and Larry, and asked what he knew about it. And guess what? Larry's dad was *not* trying to persuade the coach that Larry is a better player. He's worried about Larry's attitude. Larry asked his father to persuade the coach to make him the starter, but Joe told Larry he wouldn't and that he didn't think Larry was going about this the right way. Understand? Joe wasn't talking about *you*. He was talking about his own son, and asking Coach Bodie what he should do."

Keith was surprised. "He . . . he *was?* But I thought . . ."

"I know what you thought, Keith. But it turns out you were wrong. Is it possible you were wrong about anything else?"

"Anything else? Like what?" Keith suspected he already knew what.

"Oh . . . maybe whether Heck is still your friend, despite your suspicions, or whether Coach Bodie and the team still want you, despite your suspicions . . . stuff like that. And, of course, about how you treat your sister."

"I *said* I was sorry," Keith mumbled, feeling ashamed of himself.

"I'd go tell her again and make sure she's all right. The other thing I wish you'd do is try to figure out why what happened to you almost a year ago is still so important to you. Why is it making you suspect your friends, yell at your sister? Why is it keeping you from enjoying a game you used to love?"

Keith looked at his feet. "I don't know."

Mr. Stedman said, "I'll bet you might work it out, if you really think it over."

"Well . . . I'll try. Now I better see Traci."

Keith's father smiled. "Good idea."

Keith found Traci in her room. She looked at him as though she wasn't sure how he was going to behave. "Trace, I'm real sorry about what happened at dinner. I was wrong to yell at you, and I'll try to never do it again."

Traci gave him a bright smile. "Okay." The smile changed to a look of concern. "How come you're feeling so bad?"

Surprised, Keith asked, "How do you know how I'm feeling?"

"'Cause I heard you yell last night, like you were having a real bad dream. The kind of bad dream I used to get."

"You 'used to get'? You mean you don't get bad dreams anymore?" Keith found himself interested.

"Oh, sure I get them," his sister replied. "But

they're not so bad, and they go away." She shrugged. "Mommy says the worst dreams are all just pretend. So when I have a really bad dream I tell myself it's all just pretend and I don't have that dream anymore."

"Huh," Keith said. "That's Mom's advice? And it works?"

Traci flopped back on her bed and nodded. "Yep. She says things you dream are much scarier than what really happens."

Keith stood up and smiled. "You know what? Maybe I've been scaring myself too much lately. Maybe I ought to stop doing that."

Traci looked at him very seriously. "It's bad to scare yourself. Unless you're just doing it for fun, like Halloween stuff."

Keith leaned over and ruffled Traci's hair. "I'm glad I talked to you. I think I can stop myself from having those bad dreams, if I work at it."

Traci grinned. "Good. Then you won't be such a grouch."

"Right," answered Keith. "Thanks for the tip, Trace. You really helped me."

He left his sister's room, wondering if it could be as simple as that.

11

Keith got to school early the next morning, hoping to have a chance to talk with Heck and straighten things out. Five minutes before he had to be in his first class, he spotted his friend in the hall and dodged between groups of students until he caught up to him.

Heck's expression was cold at first. "What do you want?"

"To say I'm sorry. I know it seems like I'm saying this a lot these days, but. . . . Well, I've been totally out of control and saying and doing really dumb things. And I'll understand if you don't want to have anything to do with me now, but I think I may be okay again, and I want to go to practice and get back to normal."

Heck was startled and a little suspicious. "Huh.

What happened? How come you're normal all of a sudden?"

Keith smiled. "Someone straightened me out."

"Yeah?" Heck was interested in spite of himself. "Who? Your dad?"

"Nope. Traci."

Heck gaped, amazed. "Your *kid sister* straightened you out? Get out of here!"

Keith laughed. "No, really. She told me — uh-oh, we better get to class. I'll explain later. But are we all right now? I really am sorry about going off like I did."

Heck shrugged and stuck out his hand. "I guess so. I mean, we have to be friends, because otherwise I'll never hear how little Traci straightened you out."

The two boys parted, friends again.

That afternoon, Keith and Heck arrived at practice together. "I better see Coach Bodie," said Keith.

"Should I come with you?" Heck asked.

"No, I'd better talk to him myself." Keith licked his lips, feeling nervous. "Then, I'm going to talk to Larry."

Heck looked doubtful. "You sure that's a good idea?"

"No," Keith admitted. "But I have to try. Maybe we can work it out that way."

"Good luck," Heck said as Keith walked away to see the coach. Coach Bodie and Mack, his assistant, were talking when Keith approached. Keith waited until the coach turned toward him.

"Yes, Keith? What's up?"

Keith cleared his throat, which suddenly felt dry. "Um, about yesterday. I know I was out of line and I shouldn't have blown up like I did. I won't let it happen again."

"Good. I would hate to lose you," the coach said. "We'll be starting in a few minutes, if you want to warm up a little."

Keith nodded and looked around, hoping that Larry was available, even though he wasn't looking forward to the conversation.

He saw Larry tying a shoe and walked over. When the other boy saw Keith coming, he stood up and stared at him with suspicion clear in his face. "What do *you* want?" he asked.

85

"First off, I'm sorry I got in your face yesterday," Keith said.

Larry didn't look any less hostile. "Well, you *should* be."

"But I don't think you should be going around bad-mouthing me to the other guys. What I did yesterday was wrong, but so is what you've been doing."

"I haven't been —" Larry started.

"Come on," Keith interrupted. "I *know* you have. I know what you said to Heck, and I've seen you talking to other players. I know you're telling them the same thing. That I'm going to choke and hurt the team."

Larry must have realized that there was no point in denying it. "Well, it's the truth! You will!"

"I don't think so," retorted Keith, sounding more certain than he was. "But the thing is, you shouldn't talk about me behind my back. It hurts the team. Think about it."

Without giving Larry a chance to reply, Keith walked away, resisting the temptation to turn around and see how the other boy was taking it.

That day, Keith decided not to think about anything other than his own work and what he could do to improve it. He was happy with his defense, knocking down a few passes — two intended for Larry — and making a few tackles. He felt confident that, on defense at least, he was going to be a valuable member of the Bucks.

On offense, he was *fairly* happy with his performance. He caught a bullet pass fired by Billy over the middle and made a good move to break a tackle and gain ten more yards. He also made a good catch of a pass thrown by Jason, even though there were three defenders around him.

But Keith dropped one of Billy's throws that he thought was catchable because he was thinking about running with the ball before he had it under control. And he missed a downfield block on Larry that would have freed Heck for a nice run.

As for Larry, he was definitely faster than Keith and his height gave him an edge. But he didn't make his cuts that well and was not a good blocker. Also, his defense was a question mark. At one point, he had a chance to tackle Heck at the line of scrimmage but hit him too high, around the shoulders, and Heck broke loose for a gain. He also tended to hesitate before coming in on running plays.

Late in the practice, Keith was on offense. Jason called for him to run a slant pattern over the middle, ten yards deep. Cody, on defense, got a hand on the ball, deflecting it slightly. Seeing it wobble off target, Keith broke back toward the line, dived, and scooped the ball up before it hit the ground.

"Great catch!" Jason shouted, running up to Keith and pulling him to his feet. As Keith got up, he saw Larry glare at Jason. Heck, who was standing behind Larry, gave Keith a thumbs-up sign.

The coach said nothing to indicate whether he favored either receiver. At the end of practice, he called the team together.

"Good work today. We're looking better, more like a team. Next week we play our first game of the year. I've arranged for us to meet with the Pumas for a scrimmage on Monday, so we can get a taste of game conditions. Afterward, I'll have a much better idea who I'll be starting on game day. Get some rest, and keep it up, everyone."

As they walked home, Heck asked Keith, "How did your talk go with Larry?"

Keith shook his head. "I'm not sure, but at least I didn't see him doing any whispering today."

"I guess the scrimmage will be the big test for us," Heck said.

"You bet," agreed Keith. He was determined to make his performance in the scrimmage prove that he deserved to start.

12

On the day of the scrimmage with the Pumas, Coach Bodie got the team together for a last meeting. "Okay, here's how this is going to work. The Puma coach and I worked it out last night. Each team is going to have ten plays on offense, starting with the ball on their own twenty. Then we switch. The Pumas will have their offensive series first.

"There won't be any official score, and if a team *does* get a touchdown or kick a field goal before its quota of plays is used up, it starts from the twenty again. Any questions?"

Players looked around at each other, and finally Cody put up his hand. "Coach? Who's going to start?"

The coach grinned. "I was just getting to that. Before I tell you, though, I want to make something clear. No matter who starts, *everyone* will get play-

90

ing time. And the fact that someone starts today doesn't necessarily mean that person will start in games."

The coach then named the starting eleven. Some, like Billy, Heck, and Cody, were obvious, but a few were not. When Keith heard his name called, he was careful not to let his pleasure show in his face.

Larry must have shown something, however, because Coach Bodie said, "Is there a problem, Larry?"

Everyone turned to look at Larry, whose face got very red. "I . . . it . . . you . . . no, no problem."

The coach nodded. "Good. I think it's a good thing that a player wants to be a starter. But when it doesn't work out that way, the thing to do is accept it and go on from there. Like I said, everyone will play, and everyone can make a contribution. Understood?"

Larry blinked and said, "Yeah," very softly. Keith was surprised to find that he felt sorry for the other boy, who wanted that starting position so badly. He hoped that if Larry turned out to be the starter in the first game, he, Keith, would be a better sport about it.

The Pumas, wearing red shirts to distinguish

themselves, lined up. Keith, in the Buck secondary, positioned himself opposite a receiver who was split wide to the left. The Puma quarterback spun and handed off to his upback, and Keith ran in toward the line to help on the stop. His help wasn't needed, though, since Cody met the runner head-on for no gain.

On the next play, the quarterback faked a pitchout and dropped back. The receiver that Keith was covering, a wiry, long-legged guy, pretended he was making a downfield block on Keith, then tried to sprint past him. Keith didn't bite on the feint and wheeled to run with the receiver, staying with him pretty well. The quarterback threw just as the Puma end put on the brakes and hooked back toward the line. Keith hit him just after the ball did and jarred the ball loose for an incomplete pass.

A few plays later, Larry replaced Keith, who got an approving nod from Coach Bodie and Mack as he reached the sideline. Keith feared that Larry wouldn't be able to keep up with this receiver, who was shifty and had a deceptive burst of speed. Sure enough, two plays later Larry stumbled in an effort to stay with his man and the Puma caught a pass and raced downfield for fifteen yards before being tackled from behind by Billy.

But on the very next play, Larry was able to break up an attempted screen pass and almost intercept it. If he had held the ball, he might have run it back for a touchdown.

The Pumas failed to score in their ten plays and the Bucks took over. Larry, who had stayed in the game, caught a short pass on the first play. A moment later, his block set up a long run for Heck. Keith joined his teammates in cheering. He was eager to get into the game again, and two plays later he did, along with Jason, who substituted for Billy.

Jason called for Keith to cut over the middle and fired a pass that was slightly behind him. Keith managed to twist around and get a hand on the ball, but a hard hit knocked it away from him, and Keith sprawled on the turf.

As he returned to the huddle, Jason said, "Sorry, dude. That was my mistake."

Keith hoped that it looked that way to Coach Bodie as well. With three plays left, Jason sent Keith long and hurled the ball as far as he could. Keith sprinted hard for the end zone, hoping to reach the pass, and reached out a hand as he crossed the goal line. He got his fingertips on the ball, knocked it upward, then cradled his arms under the ball, catching it in both hands as he fell forward for a touchdown. As he got to his feet, he was surrounded by teammates slapping his hands and yelling congratulations.

On the last offensive play, Billy, back in at quarterback, called an end around. Keith used Cody to run interference and raced for a twenty-yard gain.

The Pumas did score on their next set of plays, but the Bucks scored a second touchdown — on some fine open-field running by Heck — and also kicked a field goal. Keith felt that he'd done pretty well, especially his one spectacular TD catch. But, he decided, Larry had also done well, even making an interception to end a Puma scoring threat.

Afterward, once the members of both teams had shaken hands and the Pumas had left, Coach Bodie assembled the Bucks.

"I'm very encouraged by what you guys showed me today. We look like we're about ready for the season opener. I'll be polishing some things in the next few practices, and that's about it.

"As for a final decision on starters, I'll sleep on it and let you know before we go to work tomorrow. For what it's worth, you've made some of my choices hard to make. That's a good problem for a coach. It means that we have some real depth on the team this year, more so than last season. Get your rest, and I'll see you all at the usual time."

Keith, Cody, and Heck rode their bikes home after the coach dismissed the team. Cody turned to Keith and said, "It's a lock, man. You're the starter. No question anymore."

Keith shrugged. "I'm not totally sure. To tell you the truth, I thought Larry had a good scrimmage, too. He made a couple of really good plays."

"That's true," Heck said, "but he also made a couple of mistakes, especially on defense. I think Cody's right."

"Sure, I'm right!" Cody insisted. "Keith, you're da *man!*"

"Well, anyway, you two guys are going to start," Keith said. "And I guess we'll know about me tomorrow."

It was going to be a long wait.

13

The next day, Keith arrived at practice feeling nervous. Heck kept reassuring Keith that he deserved to start for the Bucks and that the coach could be relied on to make the right decision. But Keith couldn't get over his edginess.

What if Coach Bodie held Keith's temper tantrum of a few days ago against him? What if the coach believed that Keith might actually fail in a clutch situation? What if, what if. . . . Keith refused to let himself relax. He promised himself that if the coach picked Larry over him he would *not* show his disappointment, that he'd still do his best for the team, and that he'd congratulate Larry and shake his hand.

When, at last, Coach Bodie blew his whistle and clapped for the team to gather around him, Keith thought that he couldn't stand the suspense for another minute. *Anything* would be better than waiting. He had to know.

The coach waited for all the whispering and talking to die down before saying a word. Then he said, "As I said yesterday, I had a few difficult decisions to make, because we can only start eleven players. In a couple of cases, there was almost nothing separating the two options, but I had to make the choice anyway.

"I'll say this again: All of you will play against the Mustangs. They're a solid team; they have a larger squad than we do, and that means that we'll need to keep moving fresh bodies out there. Here we go."

He read the names off a list, going through them quickly. When he said, "Keith Stedman," Keith wasn't sure at first that he'd heard right. Then he saw Heck nodding and grinning, and he knew that he had indeed heard right. He was on the starting team! He managed not to jump up and let out a whoop, but he felt really *good*.

In addition, he felt a tingle of nervousness. Now he had what he wanted. It was put-up-or-shut-up time.

What if he blew it . . . *again*? What would he do?

Meanwhile, the coach was talking about running some new plays and drilling all the old ones, and Keith made an effort to follow it all, but found it hard to focus.

As soon as Coach Bodie told the players to take a minute before they got to work, Keith headed straight for Larry, who was sitting on the ground and staring hard straight ahead of him. "Hey, Larry?" Keith called.

The other boy looked up, and Keith stuck out his hand. "Larry, I hope there's no hard feelings. I thought we looked pretty much dead-even lately, and it could have gone either way. And I figure you'll get plenty of playing time."

Larry got to his feet and forced a smile onto his face. "Congratulations," he said. "I guess you earned it. Anyway . . . well, good luck."

Keith thought that if it had been the other way around, he'd probably have had just as much trouble getting the words out.

As practice went on, Keith noticed that Larry's head didn't seem to be in it at all. At one point, when Larry was on offense, Billy must have called for the receiver to cut toward the sideline, because that's where he threw the pass. But the ball landed ten yards from any player, while Larry raced straight downfield. As he headed glumly back to the huddle, the coach glared at him, but didn't say anything. Keith was sure that it was because Coach Bodie knew how Larry was feeling and wanted to cut him a little slack.

Keith felt *pumped*. He couldn't do anything wrong. One of Jason's passes was tipped at the line of scrimmage and Keith somehow leaped over a couple of players to grab it before it hit the ground. He made a beautiful ankle-high tackle on Heck when it seemed that Heck was going to take it into the end zone. He hoped that he'd have this kind of feeling when game time rolled around.

When the coach whistled play to a halt, Keith felt that he could keep going and going, like one of those batteries in TV commercials. "Keith, Larry, let me see you for a minute," the coach called.

Heck looked at Keith with a "What's up?" expression, but Keith could only shrug. He had no idea.

"Guys, with you two playing as well as you are, I'd

like to put in a new play, a spread formation kind of thing, with both of you in the lineup and Heck in the slot. Here's the idea."

He kneeled down, holding a clipboard with a penciled diagram on it. Keith caught Larry's eye and grinned. Larry grinned back.

"The thing would be to flood the secondary," Coach Bodie said. "One of you two would go deep down one sideline, the other would cut across maybe fifteen yards out. Heck would be flanked, ready for a screen pass or something short. Billy has great peripheral vision and he could decide which man is most open. If, say, we're behind with time running out, or if it's a close game and we want to catch them by surprise, this could be a real weapon."

Keith looked at the coach and then at Larry. "Sounds great."

Larry asked, "When are we going to work on it?"

"Tomorrow," the coach replied. "I don't know if we'll use it right away, but I'd like to be able to if we want it. Take a couple of minutes, and then we'll get back to work."

Keith and Larry nodded. Heck came up to Keith

as soon as Keith was far enough away so that Larry wouldn't hear their conversation.

"What was *that* about?" he asked.

Keith hesitated, and then said, "Well, the coach didn't ask us to keep it a secret so I don't see why I can't tell you. He has a new play he wants to put in tomorrow, with Larry and me together."

Heck's eyes lit up. "Yeah?"

Keith nodded. "You'd be a flanker. We'd have three receivers in the pattern and Billy would decide which of us to throw to. Coach called it a kind of spread formation."

"Like the pros use!" Heck was excited about the idea. "Come on, let's tell Billy!"

"Looks like the coach is doing that already," Keith said, pointing to where the coach was talking to Billy and Jason, who were looking at the coach's clipboard. "He'll probably show it to you, too, before we finish up today."

"A pro set!" Heck repeated. "How fantastic is *that!?*"

"Think we could make it work?" asked Keith. "It looks kind of complicated."

"With Billy at quarterback?" Heck exclaimed.

101

"Sure we can! The other team won't know what hit them!"

Keith spent the rest of the day's workout looking forward to the next day, and hoping he could do his part.

14

When Mr. Stedman got home that evening, Keith was waiting for him eagerly. As he opened the door, Keith ran up.

His father looked at him anxiously for a moment. "Anything wrong?"

"Wrong? No! Everything's great! Well, maybe not great, exactly, but good, at least I *think* it's good. Well, I *hope* it's good, but I'm not sure yet, because —"

"*Ho!* Slow down, there!" called Mr. Stedman, laughing at Keith's excitement. "I'm having trouble following this. First of all: Does this mean that there are no problems as far as football is concerned?"

"Uhn-uhn, no problems. . . . Well, we have only two practices before we play the Mustangs and I'm nervous, but that's okay, it's not a problem, really."

"All right, then." Keith's father relaxed a little. "Everything is settled as far as Larry goes, then?"

"Oh, sure!" Keith grinned. "Coach says I'm going to start and I shook hands with Larry and there are no hard feelings, even though he's disappointed, but he stopped talking about me behind my back, and —"

"Tell you what," said his father, smiling now that he understood that Keith's news was good, "let me sit down and catch my breath, and you can tell me all about it. But *slowly*, all right?"

Keith and his father sat down together in the den, where Keith explained Coach Bodie's new play. "It's a winner! I think it's going to catch the Mustangs totally by surprise. They won't know how to cover us when we send out all those receivers, and Billy is going to pick their defense apart!"

Mr. Stedman laughed. Keith stopped, staring at his father suspiciously. "What's so funny?"

"Nothing's funny," Mr. Stedman assured his son. "I'm just relieved that tonight's football news is *good* for a change, that's all."

"Oh." Keith took a breath and sat back. "Yeah, I guess I was pretty down for a while. But that's over now. I think. I'm pretty sure."

"Well, that's very good, son. What happened to change your attitude? Just wondering."

"It was something Traci said when I went in to apologize to her the other night. She was talking about how she got over the nightmares she was having. She realized that things are almost never as bad in real life as they are in your dreams. And it was the same for me. I was making everything much worse than it really was, and when I saw that . . . well, I just, sort of . . . settled down."

"Well, well," Mr. Stedman said. "Thanks to Traci. Did you tell her?"

"I will tonight," Keith replied. "I really owe her."

"She's going to be very happy to hear that she helped you," said Keith's father. "She really loves you. I guess you knew that already."

"Sure," Keith said, "but maybe I needed to be reminded."

The next afternoon, while Mack ran through some blocking drills with the interior linemen, Coach Bodie took the backs and ends aside to teach them his spread formation offense.

"Now, I don't know for sure that we'll use this against the Mustangs tomorrow, but it'll be good to have it available. And I'm pretty certain we'll get around to using it sooner or later this season."

He unfolded a big sheet of paper covered with diagrams.

"Looks complicated," Billy said, staring at the paper.

"Not really," the coach assured him. "There's one basic formation and a few different variations where the receivers take different routes. For tomorrow, though, to make matters simpler, I think we'll just concentrate on one version."

It *was* pretty simple, Keith decided. He lined up wide right, with Larry on the same side a few yards closer to the interior line. Heck was a flanker, also on the right but a few yards behind the line. The fullback stayed in the backfield to block. On the snap, Keith would run a fly pattern, streaking straight downfield. Larry would cut across the middle, fifteen yards deep. Heck would cut sharply for the sideline, only a few yards downfield. Interior linemen, including Cody, would screen block on the line and try to create a downfield convoy of blockers for Heck, so that he might pick up additional running yards if the ball were thrown to him.

The coach had different combinations of receivers try it out without linemen at first, using both Billy and Jason at quarterback. Jason was a little confused in the beginning and had trouble picking out the various receivers, but soon adjusted. Billy had no difficulty at all, and threw to Keith, Larry, and Heck in turn. After twenty minutes, the coach was satisfied.

"Now let's run it with linemen," he said. He signaled for Mack to bring the rest of the team over.

Cody and the rest of the linemen seemed to grasp their assignments quickly, and the coach began to run plays from the spread formation. On the first one, Keith faked as if he were going to cut toward the sideline and then dashed downfield. Billy fired the ball deep and Keith looked back, saw it coming — and dropped the pass. Disgusted with himself, he kicked at the ball before picking it up and running it back to the line. He flipped it to Billy, turned to Coach Bodie, and said, "The pass was perfect and I blew it. Sorry."

"Don't worry about it," said the coach. "That's what practice is for."

Larry, Keith noticed, said nothing to anyone.

Heck patted Keith on the shoulder and said, "You'll get it next time."

And that was that. Keith was mildly surprised that not only did nobody make anything of his drop, but that he himself felt only a slight irritation at his goof.

The practice went on, with Billy throwing to Larry, Keith, and Heck, after which Coach Bodie brought Jason in. Jason threw a long pass to Keith, who caught it over his shoulder without breaking stride.

"All *right!*" yelled Heck.

"Way to go!" called Larry.

The coach just smiled and said nothing, and Keith felt great.

After running a few more plays from the formation, Coach Bodie looked at his watch and blew his whistle.

"Good work today. Get your rest and go over your assignments, and let's go out and play some tough football tomorrow."

Keith found himself exchanging a look with Larry.

"That's a killer play," Larry said after a moment.

Keith grinned. "The Mustangs are in trouble."

15

The first game of the season was minutes away. The weather was perfect for football, cool and clear with almost no wind. Keith remembered the first game the previous year, and he had the same sensations now. There was a tingly feeling in his belly and he was nervous, but not frightened. He thought that the nervousness would disappear as soon as play began.

The stands were fairly full, with rooters for both teams on hand. Keith's family was sitting with Heck's folks, and Mr. Szymanski had Heck's baby brother in his lap. The Mustangs, in their sky-blue-and-gray uniforms, were warming up at one end of the field, while the starting Buck team, wearing black and silver, ran off some snaps at the other end. The opposing coaches and the two game officials were conferring at midfield.

Heck said, "This is my brother's first game. Let's win it for him, okay?"

Keith laughed. "If you say so. I was planning to win it for my sister. How about splitting it — half for Traci and half for little Stan?"

He noticed Traci waving to him and waved back.

The Bucks won the coin toss and elected to receive. They crowded around their coach, who advised them, "When we go on defense, remember that the Mustangs had a terrific running game last year and their top runner is back. He's big and strong and he doesn't get tired, so be ready for him. Make them go to the passing game if you can.

"As for our offensive attack, you're ready for them. I think we can use our passing to spread them out, and then we can do some serious running." He looked around at the players and asked, "Are we ready for this one?"

"*YEAH!*" the Bucks yelled. They took the field, with Heck as the deep man to receive the kickoff. He fielded the kick on the fifteen and, with a particularly solid block from Cody, ran it back to the Bucks' forty.

Billy called for a first-down pass, sending Keith wide to the left. He faked a handoff to Heck and threw a bullet pass that reached Keith just as he made his cut. The play gained twelve yards. Another pass, this one to Heck in the flat, was set up by some good blocking. Keith drove a Mustang linebacker back several yards and Heck gained nine. The ball was on the Mustang thirty-nine, and the Buck fans were on their feet, yelling encouragement.

Another pass to Keith, running a sideline pattern, brought the ball down to the eighteen. The Mustang coach, sensing that his team was confused, called a time-out.

When play resumed, Billy sent Keith into the end zone but handed off to Heck. Heck darted through a nice hole formed by the blockers and made it to the four-yard line before being stopped. Billy then kept the ball on a bootleg, sprinting around right end for a touchdown.

But the coach had been right about the Mustang running game. Following the kickoff their star player, a tall halfback, began ripping off big chunks of yardage, and the Mustangs moved the ball into Buck territory. Keith came out, replaced by Larry.

As he passed Larry, Keith said, "That runner of theirs is tough — don't try to tackle him high. Hit him low or he'll just drag you or shake you off." Larry nodded and raced on.

Keith stood next to Heck on the sideline. "That back is humongous," he said, and Heck nodded.

"Maybe he'll get tired," he said.

"Maybe . . . and maybe *we'll* get tired trying to stop him," Keith replied, as the Mustang runner gained another eight yards up the middle, with three Bucks draped all over him.

Finally, the Mustang quarterback tried a pass. Cody almost tackled him in the backfield, so the pass was rushed and incomplete. The Mustang half-back then raced to his right, as if making an end run, but handed off to an end on a reverse, catching the Buck defense by surprise. Untouched, the Mustang receiver sped into the end zone. The extra point was good, and the score was tied at 7 apiece as the first quarter ended.

On their next offensive series, the Bucks made

some good yardage, with Jason at quarterback. He found Larry for a nice gain, and then hit Heck for another ten yards. But the drive stalled on the Mustang eight, so the Bucks had to settle for a field goal, putting them ahead, 10–7.

The Mustangs were able to grind out more yardage when they got the ball. On one play, Keith met the Mustang halfback head-on as he moved in from his position in the secondary to plug a hole — he thought. The runner lowered his head and Keith bounced backward, grabbing desperately onto a leg as the back charged forward. With the help of three other Bucks, including Heck, the guy was finally brought down. The quarterback tried another pass, but Billy blitzed from his safety position, catching the opposing QB for a ten-yard loss.

The Mustangs, however, tried and converted a twelve-yard field goal and tied the score at 10.

Late in the half, Billy made a mistake and forced a pass to Heck in the flat. A Mustang defender picked it off. There was nobody between him and the end zone. He ran back the interception for a touchdown, giving the Mustangs a 17–10 lead. Billy was furious at himself for his error, but Keith and the other Bucks urged him not to be too hard on himself.

"We'll get it back," Keith promised.

There was less than a minute left in the first half when the Bucks went back on offense. Heck made a nice gain over tackle, with a strong downfield block from Larry, who was in as a receiver. On third down, with the ball at midfield and the clock showing only a few seconds left, Billy threw long for Larry, who raced past his defender. Larry reached for the ball, juggled it for one second, and lost the handle as the clock ran out. Shocked and unhappy, Larry slowly walked off the field, staring at the ground.

Keith ran up to the unhappy Buck. "Don't let it get to you," he said. "We have another half to win this game."

But Larry was miserable. "I should've had it. I *did* have it. . . . And I lost it. I just got . . . I don't know, panicky, like everything was on my shoulders, and I froze. I choked."

"It's no big deal. Don't blame yourself," Heck urged.

"Larry, I've *been* there," Keith pointed out. "It

was just a physical mistake. Remember what Coach Bodie says about those. Come on, don't beat yourself up. We *need* you for the second half."

Larry took a deep breath and managed a shaky smile. "Thanks. Now I know what it — Okay, I'm all right."

Keith slapped him on the shoulder.

During the halftime break, Coach Bodie said, "We can win this. I can't believe that runner of theirs can keep this up for another half. He's got to wear down, and they don't have too many other weapons. I want to use the halfback option in the second half. Heck, you decide whether to run or to throw to Keith or Larry, whoever's in at the time. And we might use that spread formation, too. Don't get down on yourselves, and we'll do what we have to."

The Mustangs received the second-half kickoff and couldn't get a first down on their first possession. Larry was clearly determined to make up for his error, and tackled the Mustang halfback in the backfield just as he took the handoff. The Mustangs were forced to punt.

On the Bucks' first offensive play, Billy threw a screen pass to Heck, who got loose for fifteen yards when Larry leveled a linebacker with a beautiful block. The coach sent Keith in for Larry, saying, "Tell Billy to use that option."

So on the next play, Billy flipped the ball to Heck, who circled to his left and looked downfield. Keith had faked a block, and when the man covering him charged to stop a possible run, he raced into the defensive backfield. Heck's pass was wobbly, but Keith caught it and rambled to the Mustang one before being tripped up. Billy kept the ball on the next play and bulled into the end zone behind Cody's charge. Following the successful point after, the score was tied at 17 all.

The two teams traded punts. As the coach had predicted, the Mustang halfback seemed to tire. The Buck defense concentrated on him, since it didn't look like they had much to worry about in the way of a passing attack.

In the middle of the fourth quarter, however, the Mustang quarterback finally found his touch. He hit his tight end, a powerfully built receiver, who took the ball down to the Buck five. At that point the

Mustang runner found some reserve energy and dived over the goal line, putting his team ahead by six. However, Cody blocked the extra-point attempt.

Neither the Bucks nor the Mustangs did much with the ball on their next possessions. The Bucks got the ball back after a Mustang punt with a little less than two minutes left, and put it in play on their own thirty-two. Heck gained five yards, and the Buck fullback picked up three. With third and two, Coach Bodie signaled for a time-out and waved Billy over for instructions.

Billy returned, bringing Larry with him, and Keith started off the field. Billy stopped him and waved him back. He gathered the team together.

"Coach wants to go to the spread offense. Guys, make your moves *fast,* because I don't have much blocking with this play. I'll find someone clear. We're going on a quick snap count, and maybe we'll catch them totally by surprise. Okay? Let's *go!*"

Keith, Larry, and Heck all came to the right side of the line. The Mustangs looked startled and confused but didn't call a time-out. Billy barked out the signals. As he took the snap, Keith took five steps downfield and made a fake toward the sideline. His

117

man hesitated. Keith raced downfield. Behind him, Larry ran a deep crossing pattern.

Seeing that Keith had outrun the defense, Billy threw a high, deep pass in his direction. For one frightening moment, Keith thought that the ball had been overthrown, but he managed to find an extra burst of speed, grabbed the ball, and pulled it in. He looked back to see Larry erase a possible tackler with a perfect block. He dashed the last ten yards into the end zone for the game-tying touchdown.

With the successful extra-point conversion, the Bucks led, 24–23.

There were still forty seconds remaining, so the Bucks went into a prevent defense, with eight men back to guard against long passes. The Mustang halfback was able to pick up some ground, but not enough to score, and the Mustangs' last two plays were desperation passes. Keith picked off the final pass and the Bucks won the game by a single point!

Keith ran off the field hugging the ball while happy teammates surrounded him, yelling and exchanging high-fives. Keith looked for his family and gave them a big, happy smile.

Heck grabbed Keith by the shoulders and spun him around. "All *right!* How does it feel, bud?"

"Totally awesome!" Keith yelled back. And that pretty much summed it up.

The nightmare was definitely over.